The European Union

Political, Social, and Economic Cooperation

The
EUROPEAN UNION

POLITICAL, SOCIAL, AND ECONOMIC COOPERATION

The European Union

Political, Social, and Economic Cooperation

SPAIN

by
Rae Simons

Mason Crest Publishers
Philadelphia

Mason Crest Publishers Inc.
370 Reed Road, Broomall, Pennsylvania 19008
(866) MCP-BOOK (toll free)
www.masoncrest.com

First printing
1 2 3 4 5 6 7 8 9 10

Library of Congress Cataloging-in-Publication Data

Simons, Rae.
  Spain / by Rae Simons.
      p. cm.—(The European Union)
  Includes bibliographical references and index.
    ISBN 1-4222-0062-0
    ISBN 1-4222-0038-8 (series)
  1. Spain—Juvenile literature. I. Title. II. European Union (Series) (Philadelphia, Pa.)
  DP17.S487 2006
  946—dc22
                                        2005007419

Design by Benjamin Stewart.
Produced by Harding House Publishing Service, Inc.
Cover design by MK Bassett-Harvey.
Printed in the Hashemite Kingdom of Jordan.

CONTENTS

THE
EUROPEAN
UNION

ICELAND ☆ Reykjavik

GREENLAND SEA

BARENTS SEA

NORWEGIAN SEA

White Sea

Oulu ☆

FINLAND

Tampere ☆ Turku

NORWAY

Trondheim ☆

Lillehammer ☆

Bergen ☆

Oslo ☆

Helsinki ☆

Gulf of Finland

Tallinn ☆

ESTONIA

Tartu

RUSSIA

Moscow ☆

SWEDEN

Stockholm ☆

Norrköping

Gulf of Riga

Ventspils ☆

LATVIA

Riga ☆

Daugavpils

DENMARK

BALTIC SEA

Liepāja ☆

Klaipėda ☆

LITHUANIA

Kaunas ☆

Vilnius ☆

Minsk ☆

UNITED KINGDOM

Glasgow ☆ Edinburgh

Belfast ☆

IRELAND

Dublin ☆

NORTH SEA

Aalborg ☆

Helsingør ☆

Odense ☆ Copenhagen ☆

Malmö ☆

RUSSIA

Gdańsk ☆

BELARUS

Hamburg ☆

POLAND

Warsaw ☆

Kyiv ☆

UKRAINE

Liverpool ☆ Manchester

Birmingham ☆

London ☆

Amsterdam ☆ **THE NETHERLANDS**

Berlin ☆

Leipzig ☆

Wrocław ☆

Kraków ☆

Košice ☆

BELGIUM

Brussels ☆

Düsseldorf ☆

Cologne ☆

GERMANY

Dresden ☆

Prague ☆

CZECH REPUBLIC

Brno ☆

SLOVAKIA

Minsk

LUXEMBOURG

Luxembourg ☆

Paris ☆

Frankfurt Main ☆

Stuttgart ☆

Munich ☆

Linz ☆

Salzburg ☆

Vienna ☆

Győr ☆

Bratislava ☆

Budapest ☆

MOLDOVA

Chișinău ☆

Sea of Azov

FRANCE

SWITZERLAND

Bern ☆

Geneva ☆

AUSTRIA

HUNGARY

Szeged ☆

ROMANIA

Bucharest ☆

BLACK SEA

Nantes ☆

Ljubljana ☆

Trieste ☆

SLOVENIA

Zagreb ☆

Venice ☆

CROATIA

Belgrade ☆

Sarajevo ☆

BOSNIA-HERCEGOVINA

YUGOSLAVIA

BULGARIA

Sofia ☆

Lyons ☆

Milan ☆

Turin ☆

Bay of Biscay

Bordeaux ☆

Toulouse ☆

Marseille ☆

Nice ☆

Florence ☆

ITALY

Rome ☆

Naples ☆

MACEDONIA

Skopje ☆

Tirana ☆

ALBANIA

Thessaloniki ☆

AEGEAN SEA

Ankara ☆

TURKEY

Vigo ☆

Bilbao ☆

Gulf of Lion

TYRRHENIAN SEA

IONIAN SEA

GREECE

Athens ☆

PORTUGAL

Porto ☆

Lisbon ☆

Madrid ☆

Barcelona ☆

SPAIN

Valencia ☆

Faro ☆

Sevilla ☆

Strait of Gibraltar

MEDITERRANEAN SEA

Kalamata ☆

Sea of Crete

Lefkosia (Nicosia) ☆ **CYPRUS**

Lemesos ☆

SY

LEBANON

Beirut ☆

Damascus ☆

JO

MALTA

Valetta ☆

Algiers ☆

Tunis ☆

MOROCCO

Rabat ☆

ALGERIA

MEDITERRANEAN SEA

Jerusalem ☆

ISRAEL & THE PALESTINIAN TERRITORIES

Amman ☆

TUNISIA

Tripoli ☆

LIBYA

Cairo ☆

EGYPT

SPAIN
European Union Member since 1986

Santander

Victoria-Gasteiz

León

Vigo

Valladolid

Zaragoza

Barcelona

Salamanca

★ **Madrid**

Castellón
de la Plana

Menorca

Mallorca

Palma

Valencia

*Balearic
Islands*

Badajoz

Ibiza

Alicante

Murcia

Córdoba

Cartagena

Sevilla

Huelva

Granada

Almeria

Málaga

Cádiz

INTRODUCTION

Sixty years ago, Europe lay scarred from the battles of the Second World War. During the next several years, a plan began to take shape that would unite the countries of the European continent so that future wars would be inconceivable. On May 9, 1950, French Foreign Minister Robert Schuman issued a declaration calling on France, Germany, and other European countries to pool together their coal and steel production as "the first concrete foundation of a European federation." "Europe Day" is celebrated each year on May 9 to commemorate the beginning of the European Union (EU).

The EU consists of twenty-five countries, spanning the continent from Ireland in the west to the border of Russia in the east. Eight of the ten most recently admitted EU member states are former communist regimes that were behind the Iron Curtain for most of the latter half of the twentieth century.

Any European country with a democratic government, a functioning market economy, respect for fundamental rights, and a government capable of implementing EU laws and policies may apply for membership. Bulgaria and Romania are set to join the EU in 2007. Croatia and Turkey have also embarked on the road to EU membership.

While the EU began as an idea to ensure peace in Europe through interconnected economies, it has evolved into so much more today:

- Citizens can travel freely throughout most of the EU without carrying a passport and without stopping for border checks.

- EU citizens can live, work, study, and retire in another EU country if they wish.

- The euro, the single currency accepted throughout twelve of the EU countries (with more to come), is one of the EU's most tangible achievements, facilitating commerce and making possible a single financial market that benefits both individuals and businesses.

- The EU ensures cooperation in the fight against cross-border crime and terrorism.

- The EU is spearheading world efforts to preserve the environment.

- As the world's largest trading bloc, the EU uses its influence to promote fair rules for world trade, ensuring that globalization also benefits the poorest countries.

- The EU is already the world's largest donor of humanitarian aid and development assistance, providing 55 percent of global official development assistance to developing countries in 2004.

The EU is neither a nation intended to replace existing nations, nor an international organization. The EU is unique—its member countries have established common institutions to which they delegate some of their sovereignty so that decisions on matters of joint interest can be made democratically at the European level.

Europe is a continent with many different traditions and languages, but with shared values such as democracy, freedom, and social justice, cherished values well known to North Americans. Indeed, the EU motto is "United in Diversity."

Enjoy your reading. Take advantage of this chance to learn more about Europe and the EU!

Ambassador John Bruton,
Head of Delegation of the European Commission, Washington, D.C.

Spain's Mediterranean coastline

THE LANDSCAPE

The land of Spain lies on an enormous penin-sula called Iberia. On a map, the Iberian Peninsula looks like a slightly lopsided square with the top bent toward the east and spread wide where it joins the rest of Europe. Florida, on the southeastern tip of the United States, is a large peninsula—but the Iberian Peninsula is a nearly four times the size of Florida. Because it's a peninsula, most of Spain's boundaries are water: the Mediterranean Sea on the south and east, all the way from the Straits of Gibraltar to the French border; and the Atlantic Ocean on the northwest and southwest. Spain also shares land boundaries with France and Andorra along the Pyrenees mountain range in the northeast, and with Portugal on the west. The southern tip of Spain's peninsula is Gibralter, which Spain **ceded** to Great Britain in 1713. Out in the Atlantic Ocean, the Canary Islands also belong to Spain, as do the Balearic Islands in the Mediterranean.

Most of the Iberian Peninsula is a high **plateau** called the Meseta Central. The plateau is rimmed with mountain ranges. A few lines of mountains dissect the plateau, as do some river valleys. Along the coast are narrow plains.

QUICK FACTS: THE GEOGRAPHY OF SPAIN

Location: Southwestern Europe, bordering the Bay of Biscay, Mediterranean Sea, North Atlantic Ocean, and Pyrenees Mountains, southwest of France

Area: slightly more than twice the size of Oregon
  total: 194,897 square miles (504,782 sq. km.)
  land: 192,874 square miles (499,542 sq. km.)
  water: 2,023 square miles (5,240 sq. km.)
There are 19 autonomous communities including the Balearic Islands and Canary Islands, and 3 small Spanish possessions off the coast of Morocco.

Borders: Andorra 40 miles (63.7 km.), France 387 miles (623 km.), Gibraltar .7 miles (1.2 km.), Portugal 754 miles (1,214 km.), Morocco (Ceuta) 3.9 miles (6.3 km.), Morocco (Melilla) 6.0 miles (9.6 km.)

Climate: temperate; clear, hot summers in interior, more moderate and cloudy along the coast; cloudy, cold winters in interior, partly cloudy and cool along the coast

Terrain: large, flat with dissected plateau surrounded by rugged hills; Pyrenees in the north

Elevation extremes:
  lowest point: Atlantic Ocean—0 feet (0 meters)
  highest point: Pico de Teide (Tenerife) on the Canary Islands—12,198 feet (3,718 meters)

Natural hazards: Periodic droughts

Source: www.ciafactbook.gov, 2005.

THE MOUNTAINS OF SPAIN

The Pyrenees form a solid wall between Spain and France. In past centuries, this natural barrier kept the two nations isolated from one another, but today international railroads and highways cross the lower land at the very eastern and western ends of the mountain range. In the middle of the Pyrenees' long backbone, however, passage is still difficult from one

One of Spain's many Majorcan ports

country to the other. In several places, the craggy peaks tower higher than 9,843 feet (3,000 meters). The highest peak in the Pyrenees, Pico de Aneto, is more than 11,155 feet (3,400 meters) high. The highest mountain on the peninsula itself—Mulhacen—is part of the Sierra Nevada that cross Spain south of the city of Granada. The Sierra Nevada Mountains are as high as the Pyrenees; Mulhacen rises to 11,253 feet (3,430 meters), and many other peaks in this range also surpass 9,843 feet (3,000 meters). Other Spanish mountain ranges are the Sierra Morena, the Sistema Iberico, the Cordillera Cantabrica, and the Sistema Penibetico.

LOWLAND REGIONS

Spain's largest lowland region is the Andalusian Plain in the southwest, a wide river valley carved by the Rio Guadalquivir. As the river nears the Atlantic Ocean, it grows wider until it flows into the Golfo de Cadiz. The Andalusian Plain lies between the Sierra Morena Mountains to the north and the Sistema Penibetico to the south. Where these two chains of mountains meet in the east, the plain narrows to an **apex**.

The Rio Ebro forms another lowland basin, contained by the Sistema Iberico to the south and west and the Pyrenees to the north and east. A few smaller river valleys are close to the Portuguese border.

Along Spain's coasts, between the mountains and the seas, are narrow strips of lowland. They are the widest along the Golfo de Cadiz, where the coastal plains join the Andalusian Plain, and along the southern and central eastern coasts. The narrowest coastal plains are along the Bay of Biscay, where the Cordillera Cantabrica Mountains rise up close to the shore.

THE ISLANDS

The Balearic Islands are in the Mediterranean, fifty miles (80 kilometers) off Spain's eastern coast. These mountainous islands are actually an extension of the Sistema Penibetico that crosses Spain's

Flora and Fauna
The variety of Spain's landscape is reflected in its flora: among Spain's trees are pines, cork-oak trees, and beech trees; its flowering plants include orchids, gentians, lavender, and rosemary.

Spain's native animals are relatively small: deer, ibex, tortoises, bats, snakes (including a venomous viper), and other small creatures; only a small number of bears, wolves, and lynxes remain. Native birds include vultures, eagles, kites, bustards, storks, and flamingos. Many other species stop off on their migration route from Europe to Africa.

Puerta de la Duquesa in Spain's Malaga Province

plateau. The islands form an ***archipelago*** with a total land area of 193 square miles (500 square kilometers). Their highest point (1,400 feet, or 2,253.1 kilometers) is in Majorca, close to the coast.

Spain's other set of islands, the Canaries, fifty-six miles (90 kilometers) off the west coast of Africa, are also mountainous, formed long ago by volcanoes. The highest peaks are in the central islands: Gran Canaria (6,398 feet, or 1,950 meters) and Tenerife (12,139 feet, or 3,700 meters).

CHAPTER ONE—THE LANDSCAPE

Rivers

Spain has about 1,800 rivers and streams, but most are relatively short; all but ninety are shorter than sixty miles (96 kilometers). Only the Tagus is more than 597 miles (960 kilometers) long. For part of each year, the shorter streams are only dry riverbeds. When they do flow, however, they are often fast **torrents** of water.

Most of Spain's major rivers have their sources in the mountains and flow westward across the plateau into Portugal, eventually emptying into the Atlantic Ocean. The River Ebro, however, flows east, into the Mediterranean. Spain's northwest coastline is broken by *rias*, narrow inlets between steep rocks, similar to Scandinavia's fjords.

Spain's major rivers include the Rio Duero, the Tagus, the Rio Mino, the Rio Guadiana, and the Rio Guadalquivir. The Guadalquivir is one of the most important, because its waters create a fertile valley that is one of Spain's richest farming areas. What's more, the Guadalquivir is Spain's only **navigable** inland waterway, making the city of Seville Spain's only inland port for ocean-going ships.

Climate

Spain's main peninsula experiences three climates: continental, maritime, and Mediterranean.

The Continental Climate

Across most of Spain's central plateau, as well as in the adjoining mountains to the east and south, the temperatures vary greatly between the winter and summer seasons. This land gets little rain, and what rain does fall (usually only 12 to 25 inches, or 30 to 64 centimeters a year) tends to evaporate, leaving the land **arid**.

The northern region and the Ebro Basin have two rainy seasons, one in spring (from April to June) and the other in fall (October to November). The southern portion of the Meseta also has spring and fall rainy seasons, but the spring one is earlier (March). In the north, the spring is the wetter time of the year, while in the south, the fall is wetter. Even during these rainy seasons, however, the rain falls unpredictably, and only once in a while.

The winters are cold and windy, while the summers are warm and cloudless. In most of the Meseta, daytime summer temperatures range between 68° and 8°F (20° and 27°C). The Ebro Basin, however, is very hot during the summer; temperatures can reach higher than 43°F (43°C).

The Maritime Climate

In northern Spain, from the Pyrenees to the northwest region, the sea moderates the weather. The winters are mild, and the summers are pleasantly warm without being hot. Abundant rain falls all year round, and the temperatures rise and fall very little. Fall (October through December) is the wettest

Spain's climate is warmed by the Mediterranean.

Spain's Costa del Sol — Coast of the Sun

season, while July is the driest month. Fog and mist are common along the northwest coast.

THE MEDITERRANEAN CLIMATE

This climatic region runs along the seaward side of the mountain ranges that run parallel to the coast, reaching from the Andalusian Plain along the southern and eastern coasts, up to the Pyrenees. The total annual rainfall in this region is lower than anywhere else in Spain, falling mainly in the late fall and winter. This region is warmer than most of the rest of Spain, both in the winter and summer, with low humidity. January temperatures average 50° to 55°F (10° to 13° C), while in July and August, the temperatures average 72° to 88°F (22° to 31°C).

Winds from North Africa blow over the Mediterranean region. Referred to as the Leveche

Protecting the Environment
Like all countries, Spain has environmental problems including deforestation, soil erosion, and sea pollution. The huge success of the tourist industry has brought more pollution to Spain. Five national parks and hundreds of protected areas and reserves, however, have been established over the years.

winds, these hot, dry air currents sometimes carry fine dust from Africa. A cooler wind from the east, the Levante, funnels between the Sistema Penibetico Mountains and North Africa's Atlas Mountains.

Spain's geography and climate have helped shape the nation it is today. They also played a role in this nation's ancient history.

Fuengirola Castle in Malaga Province is a reminder of Spain's ancient history.

2 SPAIN'S HISTORY AND GOVERNMENT

CHAPTER

Archeologists have found evidence that humans have lived on the Iberian Peninsula for thousands of years. Evidence of **Neanderthal** humans has been found on

Gibraltar dating back 50,000 years, and modern humans arrived on the scene somewhere between 8000 and 4000 BCE, when the Iberians moved into Spain from the east. The Phoenicians sailed in from the east, creating trading posts along Andalucia's seaboard. Later, around 800 BCE, the Celts (the same people who settled Ireland and Scotland) arrived in the northern third of the peninsula. By 500 BCE, the Carthaginians from Northern Africa had colonized what is now southern Spain.

SPAIN AND THE ROMAN EMPIRE

In 206 BCE, the Roman Empire invaded Spain. The Roman soldiers easily crushed the native resistance and soon transformed the Iberian Peninsula into one of Rome's richest and most organized colonies. The Romans built paved roads that crisscrossed the peninsula, and they sailed their **galleys** up the Guadalquivir, all the way to Cordoba, where they loaded olive oil and wine into their holds for exportation to Rome.

When the Roman Empire adopted Christianity in the fourth century ce, Spain also became a Christian land. The Roman influence was strong on Spanish culture, and today's modern Spanish language still holds strong echoes of Rome's Latin.

THE VISIGOTHS AND THE MOORS

When the Roman Empire collapsed in the fifth century, waves of **barbarian** tribes swept across Europe. The Visigoths, a warlike Germanic people who migrated from central Europe, eventually took control of Spain.

Their rule was chaotic and disorganized, however, and eventually, in 711, the Moors swept in from Northern Africa. These Muslim people ruled the Iberian Peninsula for more than seven centuries. As Europe's Christian nations grew in power, however, they gradually drove the Moors further and further south. The last Moorish kingdom, Granada (the eastern half of modern-day Andalusia), fell in 1492 to the Catholic monarchs Isabella and Ferdinand. The Moors' cultural legacy can still be seen in Spain, especially in monuments such as the Mosque of Cordoba and the Alhambra Palace in Granada.

SPAIN AND THE NEW WORLD

Spain played an important role in the discovery of new land on the other side of the Atlantic, since King Ferdinand and Queen Isabella were the sponsors of Christopher Columbus's voyage of exploration. Columbus was followed by the **conquistadors**, who brought great wealth from the New World to Spain. As the conquistadors conquered more and more of the Americas' Native people, Spain built a vast overseas empire.

Map of old Spain

Spain became one of the strongest and most important nations in the world.

Much of the wealth Spain gained from the Americas was spent on wars with northern Europe and with the Ottoman Turks in the Mediterranean region. Gradually, the flow of riches from the New World diminished—and so did Spain's power.

Alcazar Castle—also called the Great Ship Castle—where Ferdinand and Isabella once lived

A Decline in Fortunes

During much of the eighteenth and nineteenth centuries, the nations of Europe were at war with one another. At the beginning of this period, when the Bourbon dynasty took the Spanish throne, Spain came under France's influence for nearly a hundred years. Meanwhile, Spain's South American colonies were demanding independence.

In the nineteenth century, when Napoleon Bonaparte's army was defeated during the Peninsular War, Spain regained its indepen-dence. The years that followed, however, were filled with unrest. The Spanish people were divided into opposing groups: the country and city people, the **conservatives** and the **liberals**. Violent overthrows of the government happened frequently—but none of the new governments lasted very long.

In the Spanish-American War at the end of the nineteenth century, Spain lost the last of its colonies—Cuba and the Philippines-a loss that proved devastating to Spain's economy and politics. The resulting unrest led to a stronger working class, who, in 1931, forced King Alfonso XIII to **abdicate** his throne. Spain was declared a **republic**—but not everyone was happy about this development. Conservative reaction from both the army and the Catholic Church led to the outbreak of the Spanish civil war. At the end of the

Dating Systems and Their Meaning

You might be accustomed to seeing dates expressed with the abbreviations BC or AD, as in the year 1000 BC or the year AD 1900. For centuries, this dating system has been the most common in the Western world. However, since BC and AD are based on Christianity (BC stands for Before Christ and AD stands for *anno Domini*, Latin for "in the year of our Lord"), many people now prefer to use abbreviations that people from all religions can be comfortable using. The abbreviations BCE (meaning Before Common Era) and CE (meaning Common Era), mark time in the same way (for example, 1000 BC is the same year as 1000 BCE, and AD 1900 is the same year as 1900 CE), but BCE and CE do not have the same religious overtones as BC and AD.

war, General Francisco Franco and his **nationalist** movement took control of the country.

During World War II, Spain did not openly side with either the **Allies** or the **Axis**. Unofficially, however, Franco supported the Axis. As a result, after the war, an international **blockade** was imposed on the country. Spain was **ostracized** from the community of nations, and the Spanish economy sank even lower. Poverty became all too common across the peninsula.

The Return of Good Fortune

During the **Cold War**, Spain became strategically attractive to the United States. In the 1950s,

American army bases were built in Spain, and tourists eventually came to Spain along with the military personnel. As foreign money began to flow into Spain, a large middle class emerged, and the nation's desperate poverty diminished.

When Franco died in 1975, the transition to democracy went fairly smoothly. A democratic **constitution** was put in effect in 1978, under the symbolic monarchy of King Juan Carlos II. The young monarch resolutely prodded his nation toward **Western**-style democracy and political reform.

THE PARLIAMENTARY MONARCHY

Local Governments

Spain's 1978 constitution created regional governments, similar to states or provinces in the United States and Canada. Today, there are seventeen regions. The central federal government is giving the regional government more and more responsibility. Eventually, they will have full responsibility for health care, education, and other social programs.

Today, the Spanish constitution provides for a parliamentary monarchy. The king is a traditional hereditary monarch who acts as head of state and supreme head of the armed forces—but he is not **sovereign**. Instead, sovereign power is held by a two-chamber parliament, called the Cortes, whose members are elected by the citizens.

The Cortes is made up of the Congress of Deputies and the Senate. The Congress of Deputies is the stronger of the two bodies; it consists of three hundred to four hundred members, elected by **proportional representation** every four years (unless the king chooses to call for new elections sooner). The Senate is composed of 208 elected members and 49 regional representatives, who are also elected every four years. Its primary function is territorial representation.

Either house may set a law in motion, but the Congress of Deputies can override a Senate **veto**. This means that if a political party has a solid majority in the Congress of Deputies, they have enormous political clout. The Congress of Deputies also has the power to officially approve or reject legislation, and it acts as a check against the prime minister's power, since the Congress can vote the prime minister out of office. Each chamber of the Cortes meets in separate buildings in Madrid during two regular annual sessions from September to December and from February to June.

The members of the Spanish parliament enjoy certain special privileges: they may not be prosecuted for verbal opinions expressed in the course of their duties; they cannot be arrested for a crime unless they are caught in the actual act of committing it (and even then, the Cortes must give its consent for them to be charged or prosecuted); they are guaranteed a fixed salary and allowances for extra expenses; and they are not obliged to follow their parties' dictates when they cast their votes.

Meanwhile, the king formally convenes and dissolves the Cortes; he also calls for elections and for **referenda**. He appoints the prime minister after consultation with the Cortes, and he names the other ministers, on the recommendation of the prime minister.

Although the king does not have the power to direct foreign affairs, he has a vital role as the chief representative of Spain in international relations. The potential significance of this role has been demonstrated during the reign of Juan Carlos,

Madrid's royal palace

The modern Spanish flag

whose many trips abroad and contacts with foreign leaders have enabled the Spanish government to establish important political and commercial ties with other nations. The king also has the duty to indicate the state's consent to international treaties and, with the prior authorization of the Cortes, to declare war and peace.

While the king has a largely symbolic role, the prime minister is the actual leader of the government. The king has the title of supreme commander of the armed forces, but they are actually under the prime minister's control. Once appointed, the prime minister remains in office until he resigns, loses the support of the Congress of Deputies, or his party is defeated in the general elections.

The prime minister, the deputy prime minister, and the other government ministers make up the Council of Ministers, which is Spain's highest **executive** institution. The Council of Ministers is responsible for putting into effect government policy. It is also responsible for national security and defense. In all its functions, however, it is ultimately responsible to the Cortes. The constitution provides that none of the ministers may engage in professional or commercial activity, or hold any additional public posts. During Franco's reign, senior government officials were often leaders of the business community, which led to corruption.

Today's Spain seeks to avoid the mistakes of the past by maintaining a system of government built carefully on compromise between monarchy and democracy, with a well-structured system of checks and balances.

TERRORISM

For decades, Spain's government has been involved in a campaign against Basque Fatherland and Liberty (ETA), a terrorist organization founded in 1959 and dedicated to promoting Basque independence. The ETA has carried out numerous bombings against Spanish government facilities and economic targets. The Spanish government attributes more than eight hundred deaths to ETA terrorism since its campaign of violence began. In November 1999, the ETA ended a "cease-fire" it declared in September 1998. Since that time, ETA has conducted a campaign of renewed violence. Anti-ETA demonstrations around the country have followed each attack, demonstrating that most Spaniards, including the majority of Spain's Basque population, oppose ETA violence.

Another Spanish terrorist group is known as GRAPO. GRAPO seeks to overthrow the Spanish government and establish a Marxist state. It opposes Spanish participation in NATO and the U.S. presence in Spain, and it has a long history of assassinations, bombings, and kidnappings.

Now that Spain has taken its place in the European community, it seeks to establish the same norms of safety and security that other European Union nations enjoy. The government continues to pursue vigorous counter-terrorist policies.

Puerta de la Duquera, a popular tourist destination

3 THE ECONOMY

During the nineteenth century, when the Industrial Revolution was transforming the economies of most Western European nations,

Spain "missed the boat." Instead, while other nations were turning into modern mechanized societies, Spain was deep in social and political turmoil.

At the beginning of the twentieth century, most Spaniards lived in the country, dependent on farming. The country had few factories, and even its farms were not as productive as other West European countries'. Spain lacked technology; its financial institutions were underdeveloped; and the government failed to build the economy. The Spanish civil war wreaked further havoc on the nation's economy, and Franco did very little to help matters once he came into power.

Not until the 1950s did Spain's economy begin to grow. A second period of economic

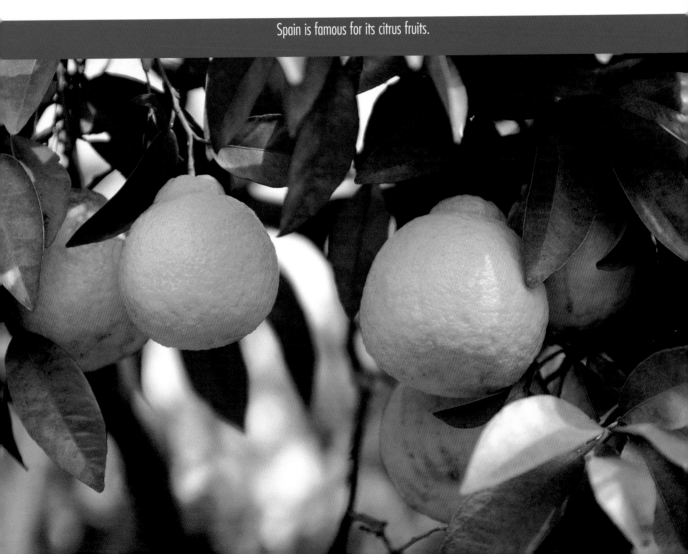

Spain is famous for its citrus fruits.

expansion began in the mid-1980s when Spain entered the European Community (EC, the forerunner of the European Union [EU]). The EC required that Spain modernize its industries, improve its **infrastructure**, and revise its economic laws to conform to EC guidelines. By doing so, Spain was able to reduce its national debt, reduce unemployment from 23 percent to 15 percent in just three years, and reduce **inflation** to less than 3 percent.

Today, Spain has been transformed from a rural backward nation of farmers into a country with a diverse economy built on strong manufacturing and service businesses. The economy of Spain is now the fifth largest in Europe, accounting for about 9 percent of the EU's total financial output. Spain's **per capita** income is 78 percent of the EU average, which is among the lowest in the EU.

EXPORTS AND IMPORTS

Spain's most important trading partners are France, Germany, and Italy. Its chief exports are machinery, including motor vehicles, and food products. The country is the world's largest producer of olive oil, the fourth largest of dried fruit, and the sixth largest of citrus fruits. Spain's vineyards are the largest in the world (60 percent larger than France's), although it's only the fourth-highest producer of wine-grapes and ranks third in wine production. Its other important crops include barley, wheat, maize, rice, potatoes, sugar beets, peppers, avocados, tomatoes, tobac-

QUICK FACTS: THE ECONOMY OF SPAIN

Gross Domestic Product (GDP): US$885.5 billion

GDP per capita: US$22,000

Industries: textiles and apparel (including footwear), food and beverages, metals and metal manufacturers, chemicals, shipbuilding, automobiles, machine tools, tourism

Agriculture: grain, vegetables, olives, wine grapes, sugar beets, citrus; beef, pork, poultry, dairy products; fish

Export commodities: machinery, motor vehicles; foodstuffs, other consumer goods

Export partners: France 19.2%, Germany 11.9%, Italy 9.7%, UK 9.4%, Portugal 9.3%, US 4.2%

Import commodities: machinery and equipment, fuels, chemicals, semi-finished goods; foodstuffs, other consumer goods

Import partners: France 16.8%, Germany 16.6%, Italy 8.8%, UK 6.5%, Netherlands 4.9%

Currency: euro (EUR)

Currency exchange rate: US$1 = .76€ (January 13, 2005)

Note: All figures are from 2003 unless otherwise noted.
Source: www.cia.gov, 2005.

co, hops, oil-bearing fruits, and cork. Meanwhile, Spain imports machinery and equipment, fuels, chemicals, food, and consumer goods.

INDUSTRIES

Just five of Spain's provinces (Barcelona, Biscay, Madrid, Navarre, and Oviedo, all located in the north and east) produce over half the country's manufacturing output. The Catalonia region, where some 85 percent of companies are located in Barcelona, is Spain's economic powerhouse and one of Europe's most important industrial regions.

Spanish industry is rooted in small and medium-sized family businesses; it has only three companies in Europe's top 100 businesses (Telefónica, Endesa, and Repsol), and another six in the top 300 (five banks, plus Berdrola). Most Spanish manufacturers are too small to compete globally. As a result, Spain has relied heavily on foreign investment (three-quarters of it in Barcelona and Madrid) for much of its recent growth. Over 30 percent of Spanish industry is foreign owned, including around 50 percent of its food production (which is mostly French owned).

The Spanish economy is hindered by its lack of modern machinery and technology; more than 90 percent of Spanish industrial plants are out of date, with machinery that needs replacing. Spain is particularly underdeveloped when it comes to computer technology, which puts the nation's industries at a definite disadvantage. Poor efficiency and lack of good business organization further weaken Spanish industries.

Spain's most important industries include tourism, chemicals and petrochemicals, **heavy industry**, and food and beverages. Its principal growth areas include tourism, insurance, property development, electronics, and financial ser-vices. Tourism is one of Spain's most important industries, especially in Andalucia.

Once the richest nation in Europe, over the past few centuries Spain has endured poverty and economic recessions. Spain's economy paid the cost for the country's isolation from the rest of the world through much of the nineteenth and twentieth centuries.

Today, despite a legacy of problems, the nation is growing economically. Tourism and **service industries** have expanded considerably. Today, only 10 percent of the population are employed in agriculture; one-third is employed by industry and service jobs account for 60 percent of all employment. Tourism accounts for approximately 10 percent of Spain's **gross domestic product (GDP)**. As it enters the twenty-first century, Spain has the world's eighth largest economy. In recent years, Spain has had an economic growth rate that is among the highest in the EU. At the same time, the country has succeeded in reducing unemployment and balancing public finances.

Yet Spain's economic difficulties linger: in spite of the fact that approximately two million new jobs were created between 1996 and 2000, the official unemployment rate remains high (approximately 13 percent of the workforce), and the inflation rate

Tourists flock to Spain's many beaches.

The town of Casares

of 3 percent in 2000 was above the EU average.

Now that Spain is a member of the EU, it has been forced to live within its means and comply with EU regulations. State spending has been slashed to control the soaring **budget deficit**. Like many modern nations, Spain can no longer afford to pay high social security benefits, and this is one of its citizens' most urgent economic worries.

With sound internal leadership, as well as guidance from the EU, Spain is working to leave behind its heritage of economic problems. Its government is revamping antiquated labor laws, working to encourage business incentives. The nation is moving into the twenty-first century on a tide of economic hope and consumer confidence.

A bullring in Ronda, Spain

4 CHAPTER

SPAIN'S PEOPLE AND CULTURE

For centuries, Spain's people lacked any true unified identity. Its regions with their varied climates and geography joined in a loose federation, but not until modern times did Spaniards begin to identify themselves with their nation rather than their particular region. Even today, Spain's regions have their own cultural, economic, and political characteristics—and people still feel that their primary loyalty lies with their town or region, and only secondarily with Spain as a whole.

SPAIN'S POPULATION GROUPS

Around the edges of the Iberian Peninsula are groups of people who have competed for centuries for control of the peninsula. The Portuguese to the west are the only group that successfully established its own state (in 1640). The Galicians live along the northwest, and the Asturians are on the northern coast of the Bay of Biscay. The Basques live near the coast toward France; the Navarrese and the Aragonese are along the Pyrenees backbone; the Catalans are in the north-

Spanish women in traditional costumes

east; the Valencians in the east; and in the south are the Andalusians.

If you asked most of these people, they would probably identify themselves by their own regional name—Basque, Valencian, Catalan, or whatever. Few of them, however, would want to **secede** from Spain. Even the Basques, where **separatist** feelings were high in the late 1980s, do not generally support total independence from Spain. (Only about one-fifth of the Basque population ever supported independence.)

RICH SPAIN AND POOR SPAIN

Economic differences make a barrier between Spaniards that's even higher than the cultural differences between the various regions. For the past century, the government has tried to redistribute the country's wealth more fairly, but these differences continue to exist.

If you drew an imaginary line from the middle of the north coast southeast to Madrid and then to Valencia, you could mark the invisible boundary that has existed between "Rich Spain" and "Poor Spain." To the north and east of the line lived the wealthy Spaniards in an area that was modern, industrial, and urban. By the 1980s, this region was already transitioning to a thriving information and services economy. But to the south and west of that imaginary line lies "Poor Spain," where most people supported themselves by farming. Social conditions here were much different from what they were on the rich side. The separation between the two groups grew even wider when the people of Rich Spain tended to think of themselves as culturally "not-Spanish."

RELIGION

Despite their differences, Spaniards have one big thing in common: almost all of them (about 97 percent) are Roman Catholic. Back in the fifteenth century, when Ferdinand and Isabella conquered Muslim Spain, they established Catholicism as the national religion. During the **Inquisition**, Jews and Muslims who refused to convert were expelled from Spain. Even those Muslims who did convert (called Moriscos) were expelled in the early 1600s. This left only the Catholics.

Today, however, few Spanish Catholics take their religion quite as seriously as Ferdinand and Isabella did. Catholic ceremonies and festivals are still vital to the flavor of Spanish culture. Though

Who Are the Basques?
The Basques are the oldest surviving ethnic group in Europe. Historians aren't sure where the Basques came from originally, but today more than 2 million Basques live in northern Spain and southwestern France. Many still speak their own language, which is unrelated to any other tongue on Earth, and they have guarded their ancient customs and traditions.

QUICK FACTS: THE PEOPLE OF SPAIN

Population: 40,280,780 (July 2004 est.)

Ethnic groups: composite of Mediterranean and Nordic types

Age structure:
  0–14 years: 14.4%
  15–64 years: 68%
  65 years and over: 17.6%

Population growth rate: 0.16%

Birth rate: 10.11 births/1,000 pop.

Death rate: 9.55 deaths/1,000 pop.

Migration rate: 0.99 migrant(s)/1,000 pop.

Infant mortality rate: 4.48 deaths/1,000 live births

Life expectancy at birth:
  Total population: 79.37 years
  Male: 76.03 years
  Female: 82.94 years

Total fertility rate: 1.27 children born/woman

Religions: Roman Catholic 94%, other 6%

Languages: Castilian Spanish 74% (official language nationwide), Catalan 17%, Galician 7%, Basque 2%

Literacy rate: 97.9% (2003)

Note: All figures are from 2004 unless otherwise noted.
Source: www.cia.gov, 2005.

For the most part, Spain's population is very **homogeneous**. The Gypsies are Spain's largest ethnic minority.

Historians surmise that the Gypsies arrived in Spain at the end of the **Middle Ages**, but no one knows for sure where they came from. The term "gypsy" comes from "Egyptian," because Europeans once believed these mysterious people came from Egypt. In fact, they probably came originally from northern India. They call themselves the Roma rather than Gypsies.

Somewhere during their long journeys, the Roma converted to Christianity. For various reasons, many began to associate the Roma with a range of negative **stereotypes**. Their **nomadic** way of life and nonconventional behaviors caused many Europeans to consider all Gypsies to be thieves, beggars, and threats to moral society.

Today, Gypsies are found in most European nations, as well as in North America. In Spain, they are spread across the country, although most

most people get married in the church, and they baptize their children, few Spaniards attend church regularly these days. They look to Catholic traditions to give their lives depth and meaning, but they tend to not seek practical direction from the Church's teachings.

Barcelona has a large Gypsy community.

Spanish Gypsy communities are in Madrid, Barcelona, and the larger southern cities. As in other countries, Spanish Gypsies have for centuries managed to preserve their own culture and social organization, based on classes and lineages. Their traditional patterns of cultural separation are increasingly difficult, however, for them to maintain in urban areas.

Recent immigration is also giving rise to new ethnic minorities in Spain. According to researchers, the level of hostility toward foreign immigrants in Spain is one of the lowest in Europe.

Spanish Arts and Culture

Architecture

Spain is famous for its architecture, particularly its Gothic churches and medieval castles. Even the smallest towns have their own distinctive architectural atmosphere. Every town and village has a plaza mayor—main square—often reached by an **arcade**. The square is usually an extended open courtyard of the town or village hall. From prehistoric monuments in the Balearic Islands to Roman ruins to fantastic modernist constructions, Spain's architecture is some of the most impressive in the world.

One of Pablo Picasso's most famous works is *Guernica* (1937), a massive painting commissioned by the Spanish government that depicts the bombing of the Basque city of Guernica. Picasso's canvas is a vivid and brutal portrayal of people, animals, and buildings wrenched by the violent bombing. The painting has become a larger symbol for the entire world, for it embodies the inhumanity and hopelessness of war.

Visual Arts

Ever since the tenth century, Spain has produced great painters. Two of the most famous are Velázquez (1599—1660) and Goya (1746—1828), who played a significant role in the evolution of painting in Europe. Works by these artists and many others can be seen at the Prado art museum in Madrid. In the twentieth century, the Spain's Paris School produced such internationally known names as Salvador Dali and Pablo Picasso.

The country is also famous for its talented craftsmen. They create carved furniture (particularly chests); tapestries and embroideries; gold, silver, and ironwork (including wrought-iron screens); sculpture; and ceramics.

Music

Spain has a rich musical heritage. The guitar was invented in Andalusia in the 1790s when a sixth string was added to the Moorish lute. By the 1870s, the guitar had gained its modern shape. Spanish musicians have taken the guitar to heights of virtuosity and none more so than Andrés Segovia (1893—1997), who established classical guitar as a musical genre.

Guitars are essential to flamenco, Spain's best-known musical tradition. Flamenco has its roots in the *cante jondo* (deep song) of the Gypsies of Andalusia, but today it is experiencing a revival. Paco de Lucia is an internationally known flamenco guitarist, and Pablo Casals is an equally gifted cellist.

Modern composers such as Enrique Granados, Isaac Albéniz, Manuel de Falla, and Joaquín Rodrigo have also gained international recognition. Placido Domingo is one of Spain's most famous operatic performers, closely followed by José Carreras. Cataluña's Montserrat Caballé is known to be one of the most outstanding sopranos in the world.

Literature

Spain's most famous author is Miguel Cervantes,

A cathedral in Barcelona is a good example of Spain's gothic architecture.

The bullfight plays a major role in Spanish culture.

who wrote *Don Quixote de la Mancha*. This seventeenth-century book is one of the earliest novels written in a modern European language, and many people consider it still to be the finest work ever written in the Spanish language.

The book tells the story of Don Quixote and his squire, Sancho Panza. Don Quixote is obsessed with stories of knights, and his friends and family think he's crazy when he sets out to wander across Spain on Rocinante, his skinny horse, righting wrongs and protecting the oppressed.

Don Quixote sees reality with the eyes of a romantic. He believes ordinary inns are enchanted castles, and peasant girls are beautiful princesses. His head-in-the-clouds dreaminess has become a part of the entire world's imagination. Even in the English language, the word "quixotic," from Don Quixote's name, means "idealistic and impractical." The expression "tilting at windmills" also comes from this story.

SPANISH PASTIMES

People in Spain love to go to the movies. They also enjoy plays, and most cities have theatres. Many of these were built by the socialist government in the 1980s and '90s.

One of the most important sports in Spain is football—or soccer, as it's called in North America. Around 300,000 spectators attend the games in the Primera División, and millions more follow the games on television. People gamble on the football results through the quiniela or football pools.

La corrida de toros—the bullfight—may be considered cruel in North American culture, but it still has a tremendous following in Spain. It gained enormous popularity in the mid-eighteenth century, when breeders developed the first breeds of *toro bravo* or fighting bulls, and it still plays a vital role in Spanish culture.

SPANISH EATING HABITS

Spaniards usually start the day with a very light breakfast (*desayuno*), often little more than coffee; they have brunch (*almuerzo*) around 10:30 A.M.; lunch (*comida*) between 1:30 P.M. and 4 P.M.; and dinner (*cena*) is as late as 10 or 11 P.M.

Cafés are the centers of social activity in most cities and villages.

Tapas are also an important part of the Spaniards' way of life. These are little snacks that include things such as *calamares* (squid), *callos* (tripe), *gambas* (prawns), *albondigas* (meatballs), and *boquerones* (anchovies) marinated in vinegar. Tapas can be taken as a meal in themselves or as a tasty bite before dinner. Each region of Spain has its own tapa specialities. Tapas bars have become popular eating places in the United States.

What Does "Tapa" Mean?
The actual translation of tapa is "lid." The story goes that bar owners used to cover drinks with a piece of bread to keep the flies away. It then became practice to put a tidbit of meat on the bread-and this evolved into the tapas of today.

For centuries, Spain has been one of the world's great cultural centers. Its ancient roots in Africa and Rome, as well as Europe, have given it a unique flavor all its own. Because of its many colonies in the Americas, today Spain's influence still reaches around the globe.

The Mediterranean Sea plays a vital role in Barcelona's commerce.

5 THE CITIES

Madrid

In the center of the Iberian Peninsula lies Madrid, the capital of Spain. Situated high on the peninsula tableland, Madrid is Europe's highest city (2,100 feet or 650 meters above sea level). A densely populated city, Madrid is also

One of Madrid's central squares

home to art galleries and other cultural centers.

Although Madrid was once thought to have been founded by Romans, historians now believe it was originally an Islamic fort, established in 854 CE. Madrid's Muslim era ended in 1085, when the region was handed to King Alfonso VI of Castile. Although its population is thought to have numbered around 12,000 at this time, the town was not considered to be a very important one.

While Madrid remained on the fringe of Spanish history, Isabella and Ferdinand united the

Castilian and Aragonese realms in 1474, creating the original nation of Spain. Isabella and Ferdinand's grandson, Carlos I, succeeded not only to the throne of Spain but also to that of the Hapsburgs, becoming Holy Roman Emperor over territories stretching from Austria to Holland and from Spain to the American colonies. But it was Carlos's son and successor, Felipe II, who made Madrid the permanent seat of the royal court in 1561.

Over the next century, as Spain's treasure was bled dry, the country's rulers retreated to Madrid, building a sumptuous fairy-tale land of palaces and elaborate cathedrals. Meanwhile, the ordinary people who lived in Madrid sank into **abject** poverty. Eventually, in the nineteenth century, the people of Madrid rose up and fought for independence. Their struggle only left the city exhausted and facing starvation.

Society in Madrid remained dominated by the rich landowners, with the poorer classes still living in the city's slums. A full one-quarter of the working population was employed as servants in wealthy households. In 1837, the government took control of Church property, which helped build a new middle class, as working people could now afford to buy land. (Unfortunately, many great art treasures were destroyed in the process.) As more money came into the city, living conditions improved; street paving, gas lighting, sewage service, and garbage collection greatly improved Madrid's appearance.

Today, a revival of artistic and cultural activity is taking place in the city. The old city center is being restored, and public transport and public housing are also being improved. Although terrorist bombings in March 2004 on Madrid's train system left two hundred people dead and more than a thousand injured, the city is heading into the twenty-first century with pride and hope.

BARCELONA

On the shores of the Mediterranean Sea on the Iberian Peninsula's northeastern coast, Barcelona is the second largest city in Spain in both size and population. It is also the capital of Catalonia, one of Spain's seventeen regional governments.

The city has a population of 1,510,000—or almost four million if the outlying areas are also included. Barcelona's inhabitants speak two official languages: Catalan and Castillian Spanish.

Barcelona has a Mediterranean atmosphere, not only because of its geographic location but also because of its history, tradition, and cultural influences. The city dates back to the founding of a Roman colony in the second century BCE. At the beginning of the nineteenth century, with the arrival of modern industries, Barcelona experienced spectacular growth and economic revival. The 1888 World's Fair was held there and became a symbol of the city's international perspective, as well as its people's capacity for hard work. Culture and the arts flourished in Barcelona.

Today, Barcelona has many faces. It is an active, modern city—with a historic **Gothic** center. The Eixample, a carefully planned "Enlargement" project, is an area of grid-like streets—while other areas of the city are a maze of narrow, medieval lanes. These contrasts add to Barcelona's charm, making it particularly attractive to tourists.

SEVILLE

Seville, located in the southeast of Spain, is a provincial capital, the seat of the regional government, including its parliament. It has more than 700,000 inhabitants, which is nearly half the population of the entire region. The city of Seville is located on the plain of the Guadalquivir River. This river can be navigated from Seville all the way to its outlet on the Atlantic coast, which makes Seville a busy port. In 1492, Seville played an important role in the discovery and conquest of America, serving as a vital link between Spain and the Americas; today, it remains one of the most active river ports of the Iberian Peninsula.

The long Moorish occupation of the Iberian Peninsula (from 711 to 1248 CE) left a permanent print on Seville. La Giralda, the tower of an important **mosque**, is the most well-known of the remaining Islamic monuments. The seventeenth

century was a period of artistic creativity in Seville. Painters such as Velázquez, Murillo, and Valdés Leal, and sculptors like Martínez Montañés lived and worked here. The city also had an important role in world literature and was the birthplace of the myth of Don Juan, the famous lover.

Twice in the twentieth century Seville has been in the spotlight of the world's attention. In 1929, it hosted the Latin American Exhibition, which left behind important improvements in the city. More recently, Expo 92 showed the world that Seville is a modern and dynamic city.

The city is also credited with the invention of tapas. More than a thousand bars in Seville offer these tasty hors d'oeuvres, and the choice is virtually unlimited—from seafood to ham and sausage, from vegetable to cheese. Many Sevillians make a meal of them, moving from bar to bar and trying one dish at a time.

GRANADA

Granada, the capital of the region with the same name, is in the eastern part of the Spanish area known as Andalusia. The city was built at the foot

A quiet street in Seville

of the Sierra Nevada Mountains where the Darro and Genil Rivers flow together.

The Moors crossed the strait of Gibraltar in 711 CE and settled in what was then a small Visigoth town perched on a hill. When Mohammed ben Nasar founded the Nasrid dynasty in 1238, the kingdom of Granada stretched from Gibraltar to Murcia. On a hill overlooking Granada, ben Nasar built the Alhambra, a sprawling palace-citadel comprised of royal residential quarters, court complexes flanked by official chambers, a bath, and a mosque.

The Triumph Arch in Barcelona

The kingdom's splendor endured until the Moors were forced to surrender Granada to the Catholic monarchs, King Ferdinand and Queen Isabella, in 1492. During the three centuries of Muslim rule, however, a rich Islamic culture had flourished in Granada, leaving the city with amazing examples of Moorish architecture. The most famous, the Alhambra, has been declared a World Heritage Site.

As the last Moorish capital on the Iberian Peninsula, Granada has a rich heritage. Its unique history has bestowed it with an artistic wealth that includes Moorish palaces and Christian Renaissance treasures. The city brims with picturesque sites: steep, narrow streets, beautiful nooks and crannies, and marvelous landscapes.

The EU flag

6

THE FORMATION OF THE EUROPEAN UNION

The EU is an economic and political confederation of twenty-five European nations. Member countries abide by common foreign and security policies and cooperate on judicial and domestic affairs. The confederation, however, does not replace existing states or governments. Each of the twenty-five member states is **autonomous**, but they have all agreed to establish some common institutions and to hand over some of their own decision-making powers to these international bodies. As a result, decisions on matters that interest all member states can be made democratically, accommodating everyone's concerns and interests.

Today, the EU is the most powerful regional organization in the world. It has evolved from a primarily economic organization to an increasingly political one. Besides promoting economic cooperation, the EU requires that its members uphold fundamental values of peace and **solidarity**, human dignity, freedom, and equality. Based on the principles of democracy and the rule of law, the EU respects the culture and organizations of member states.

HISTORY

The seeds of the EU were planted more than fifty years ago in a Europe reduced to smoking piles of rubble by two world wars. European nations suffered great financial difficulties in the postwar period. They were struggling to get back on their feet and realized that another war would cause further hardship. Knowing that internal conflict was hurting all of Europe, a drive began toward European cooperation.

France took the first historic step. On May 9, 1950 (now celebrated as Europe Day), Robert Schuman, the French foreign minister, proposed the coal and steel industries of France and West Germany be coordinated under a single supranational authority. The proposal, known as the Treaty

of Paris, attracted four other countries—Belgium, Luxembourg, the Netherlands, and Italy—and resulted in the 1951 formation of the European Coal and Steel Community (ECSC). These six countries became the founding members of the EU.

In 1957, European cooperation took its next big leap. Under the Treaty of Rome, the European Economic Community (EEC) and the European Atomic Energy Community (EURATOM) were formed. Informally known as the Common Market, the EEC promoted joining the national economies into a single European economy. The 1965 Treaty of Brussels (more commonly referred to as the Merger Treaty) united these various treaty organizations under a single umbrella, the European Community (EC).

In 1992, the Maastricht Treaty (also known as the Treaty of the European Union) was signed in Maastricht, the Netherlands, signaling the birth of the EU as it stands today. **Ratified** the following year, the Maastricht Treaty provided for a central banking system, a common currency (the euro) to replace the national currencies, a legal definition of the EU, and a framework for expanding the

The EU's united economy has allowed it to become a worldwide financial power.

EU's political role, particularly in the area of foreign and security policy.

By 1993, the member countries completed their move toward a single market and agreed to participate in a larger common market, the European Economic Area, established in 1994.

The EU, headquartered in Brussels, Belgium, reached its current member strength in spurts. In

© BCE ECB EZB EKT EKP 2002

200

© BCE ECB EZB EKT EKP 2002

100

© BCE ECB EZB EKT EKP 2002

50

© BCE ECB EZB EKT EKP 2002

The euro, the EU's currency

1973, Denmark, Ireland, and the United Kingdom joined the six founding members of the EC. They were followed by Greece in 1981, and Portugal and Spain in 1986. The 1990s saw the unification of the two Germanys, and as a result, East Germany entered the EU fold. Austria, Finland, and Sweden joined the EU in 1995, bringing the total number of member states to fifteen. In 2004, the EU nearly doubled its size when ten countries—Cyprus, the Czech Republic, Estonia, Hungary, Latvia, Lithuania, Malta, Poland, Slovakia, and Slovenia—became members.

THE EU FRAMEWORK

The EU's structure has often been compared to a "roof of a temple with three columns." As established by the Maastricht Treaty, this three-pillar framework encompasses all the policy areas—or pillars—of European cooperation. The three pillars of the EU are the European Community, the Common Foreign and Security Policy (CFSP), and Police and Judicial Co-operation in Criminal Matters.

QUICK FACTS: THE EUROPEAN UNION

Number of Member Countries: 25
Official Languages: 20—Czech, Danish, Dutch, English, Estonian, Finnish, French, German, Greek, Hungarian, Italian, Latvian, Lithuanian, Maltese, Polish, Portuguese, Slovak, Slovenian, Spanish, and Swedish; additional language for treaty purposes: Irish Gaelic.
Motto: *In Varietate Concordia* (United in Diversity)
European Council's President: Each member state takes a turn to lead the council's activities for 6 months.
European Commission's President: José Manuel Barroso (Portugal)
European Parliament's President: Josep Borrell (Spain)
Total Area: 1,502,966 square miles (3,892,685 sq. km.)
Population: 454,900,000
Population Density: 302.7 people/square mile (116.8 people/sq. km.)
GDP: €9.61.1012
Per Capita GDP: €21,125
Formation:
- Declared: February 7, 1992, with signing of the Maastricht Treaty
- Recognized: November 1, 1993, with the ratification of the Maastricht Treaty

Community Currency: Euro. Currently 12 of the 25 member states have adopted the euro as their currency.
Anthem: "Ode to Joy"
Flag: Blue background with 12 gold stars arranged in a circle
Official Day: Europe Day, May 9.

Source: europa.eu.int

Pillar One

The European Community pillar deals with economic, social, and environmental policies. It is a body consisting of the European Parliament, European Commission, European Court of Justice, Council of the European Union, and the European Courts of Auditors.

Pillar Two

The idea that the EU should speak with one voice in world affairs is as old as the European integration process itself. Toward this end, the Common Foreign and Security Policy (CFSP) was formed in 1993.

PILLAR THREE

The cooperation of EU member states in judicial and criminal matters ensures that its citizens enjoy the freedom to travel, work, and live securely and safely anywhere within the EU. The third pillar—Police and Judicial Co-operation in Criminal Matters—helps to protect EU citizens from international crime and to ensure equal access to justice and fundamental rights across the EU.

The flags of the EU's nations:

top row, left to right
Belgium, the Czech Republic, Denmark, Germany, Estonia, Greece

second row, left to right
Spain, France, Ireland, Italy, Cyprus, Latvia

third row, left to right
Lithuania, Luxembourg, Hungary, Malta, the Netherlands, Austria

bottom row, left to right
Poland, Portugal, Slovenia, Slovakia, Finland, Sweden, United Kingdom

ECONOMIC STATUS

As of May 2004, the EU had the largest economy in the world, followed closely by the United States. But even though the EU continues to enjoy a trade surplus, it faces the twin problems of high unemployment rates and **stagnancy**.

The 2004 addition of ten new member states is expected to boost economic growth. EU membership is likely to stimulate the economies of these relatively poor countries. In turn, their prosperity growth will be beneficial to the EU.

THE EURO

The EU's official currency is the euro, which came into circulation on January 1, 2002. The shift to the euro has been the largest monetary changeover in the world. Twelve countries—Belgium, Germany, Greece, Spain, France, Ireland, Italy, Luxembourg, the Netherlands, Finland, Portugal, and Austria—have adopted it as their currency.

SINGLE MARKET

Within the EU, laws of member states are harmonized and domestic policies are coordinated to create a larger, more-efficient single market.

The chief features of the EU's internal policy on the single market are:

- free trade of goods and services

- a common EU competition law that controls anticompetitive activities of companies and member states

- removal of internal border control and harmonization of external controls between member states

- freedom for citizens to live and work anywhere in the EU as long as they are not dependent on the state

- free movement of **capital** between member states

- harmonization of government regulations, corporation law, and trademark registration

- a single currency

- coordination of environmental policy

- a common agricultural policy and a common fisheries policy

- a common system of indirect taxation, the value-added tax (VAT), and common customs duties and **excise**

- funding for research

- funding for aid to disadvantaged regions

The EU's external policy on the single market specifies:

- a common external **tariff** and a common position in international trade negotiations

- funding of programs in other Eastern European countries and developing countries

COOPERATION AREAS

EU member states cooperate in other areas as well. Member states can vote in European Parliament elections. Intelligence sharing and cooperation in criminal matters are carried out through EUROPOL and the Schengen Information System.

The EU is working to develop common foreign and security policies. Many member states are resisting such a move, however, saying these are sensitive areas best left to individual member states. Arguing in favor of a common approach to security and foreign policy are countries like France and Germany, who insist that a safer and more secure Europe can only become a reality under the EU umbrella.

One of the EU's great achievements has been to create a boundary-free area within which people, goods, services, and money can move around freely; this ease of movement is sometimes called "the four freedoms." As the EU grows in size, so do the challenges facing it—and yet its fifty-year history has amply demonstrated the power of cooperation.

Europe is proud of its "bright idea," a union with economic and political power.

The EU believes that it can use its power to act as a "lighthouse" for the rest of the world.

KEY EU INSTITUTIONS

Five key institutions play a specific role in the EU.

THE EUROPEAN PARLIAMENT

The European Parliament (EP) is the democratic voice of the people of Europe. Directly elected every five years, the Members of the European Parliament (MEPs) sit not in national **blocs** but in political groups representing the seven main political parties of the member states. Each group reflects the political ideology of the national parties to which its members belong. Some MEPs are not attached to any political group.

COUNCIL OF THE EUROPEAN UNION

The Council of the European Union (formerly known as the Council of Ministers) is the main leg-

islative and decision-making body in the EU. It brings together the nationally elected representatives of the member-state governments. One minister from each of the EU's member states attends council meetings. It is the forum in which government representatives can assert their interests and reach compromises. Increasingly, the Council of the European Union and the EP are acting together as colegislators in decision-making processes.

EUROPEAN COMMISSION

The European Commission does much of the day-to-day work of the EU. Politically independent, the commission represents the interests of the EU as a whole, rather than those of individual member states. It drafts proposals for new European laws, which it presents to the EP and the Council of the European Union. The European Commission makes sure EU decisions are implemented properly and supervises the way EU funds are spent. It also sees that everyone abides by the European treaties and European law.

The EU member-state governments choose the European Commission president, who is then approved by the EP. Member states, in consultation with the incoming president, nominate the other European Commission members, who must also be approved by the EP. The commission is appointed for a five-year term, but can be dismissed by the EP. Many members of its staff work in Brussels, Belgium.

COURT OF JUSTICE

Headquartered in Luxembourg, the Court of Justice of the European Communities consists of one independent judge from each EU country. This court ensures that the common rules decided in the EU are understood and followed uniformly by all the members. The Court of Justice settles disputes over how EU treaties and legislation are interpreted. If national courts are in doubt about how to apply EU rules, they must ask the Court of Justice. Individuals can also bring proceedings against EU institutions before the court.

COURT OF AUDITORS

EU funds must be used legally, economically, and for their intended purpose. The Court of Auditors, an independent EU institution located in Luxembourg, is responsible for overseeing how EU money is spent. In effect, these auditors help European taxpayers get better value for the money that has been channeled into the EU.

OTHER IMPORTANT BODIES

1. European Economic and Social Committee: expresses the opinions of organized civil society on economic and social issues

2. Committee of the Regions: expresses the opinions of regional and local authorities

3. European Central Bank: responsible for monetary policy and managing the euro

4. European Ombudsman: deals with citizens' complaints about mismanagement by any EU institution or body

5. European Investment Bank: helps achieve EU objectives by financing investment projects

Together with a number of agencies and other bodies completing the system, the EU's institutions have made it the most powerful organization in the world.

EU Member States

In order to become a member of the EU, a country must have a stable democracy that guarantees the rule of law, human rights, and protection of minorities. It must also have a functioning market economy as well as a civil service capable of applying and managing EU laws.

The EU provides substantial financial assistance and advice to help candidate countries prepare themselves for membership. As of October 2004, the EU has twenty-five member states. Bulgaria and Romania are likely to join in 2007, which would bring the EU's total population to nearly 500 million.

In December 2004, the EU decided to open negotiations with Turkey on its proposed membership. Turkey's possible entry into the EU has been fraught with controversy. Much of this controversy has centered on Turkey's human rights record and the divided island of Cyprus. If allowed to join the EU, Turkey would be its most-populous member state.

The 2004 expansion was the EU's most ambitious enlargement to date. Never before has the EU embraced so many new countries, grown so much in terms of area and population, or encompassed so many different histories and cultures. As the EU moves forward into the twenty-first century, it will undoubtedly continue to grow in both political and economic strength.

Spain's Europa Point Lighthouse

7 SPAIN IN THE EUROPEAN UNION

After the world wars, Spain was isolated from the rest of the world. Franco's government sought to establish closer ties with Europe, and after his death, this became Spain's number-one diplomatic goal. Spain wanted to be recognized as a democratic West European society.

In 1958, Spain became an associate member of the Organisation for European Economic Co-operation (OEEC). When the Organisation for Economic Co-operation and Development (OECD) was formed in 1959, Spain became a full member. It also gained membership in the **World Bank**.

When the European Community was formed, however, it was much more reluctant to have Spain join its ranks. The member countries did not approve of the undemocratic government institutions that still existed in Spain. Finally, after six years of negotiations, a commercial trade pact was reached between Spain and the European Community in 1970, but it was an economic agreement only.

In 1977, however, Spain's first democratically elected government in more than forty years came to power. Prime Minister Adolfo Suárez González immediately sent his foreign minister to Brussels to once more ask that Spain be allowed to join the European Community. At the same time, he put into effect more democratic policies within his nation. European attitudes toward Spain began to improve, and Spain was admitted to the Council of Europe—but it was still not granted full membership in the European Community.

Negotiations for Spain's entry into the European Community were long and complicated. Even after Spain had made many democratic changes to its government, European Community members still worried about how Spain's economy would affect the European Community. Spain's economy was much less developed than that of other member nations, and its industries needed major reforms. Spanish agriculture was also much less developed than it was in the rest of Europe. Since the European Community was already in the midst of a financial crisis, its members were reluctant to take on any more economic burdens.

After lengthy bargaining, however, these issues were eventually resolved. The Treaty of Accession was signed in the summer of 1985, and on January 1, 1986, Spain finally entered the European Community. The terms of the treaty committed Spain to making major ongoing contributions to the European Community budget, but most Spaniards didn't seem to care. They had finally achieved a long-awaited goal, and now they savored being included in the West European society of nations. As the years went by, polls indicated that most Spaniards had a sense of being "citizens of Europe."

The accession agreement called for gradual integration to be carried out over a seven-year period. This adjustment transition involved a number of features:

- Customs duties were to be phased out as of March 1, 1988.

- Industrial tariffs on EC goods were to be phased out until January 1, 1993.

- Quotas on color television sets and tractors were to be eliminated by the end of 1988.

One of Barcelona's modern buildings

- Quotas on chemicals and textiles would be done away with by the close of 1989.

- Spanish workers would be able to circulate freely and seek employment in the European Community by 1993.

- Phased alignment with the European Community's Common Agricultural Policy (CAP) was to be completed only in 1996.

The Spanish regarded this last point as a **discriminatory** action taken by European Community countries to prevent the import of Spanish tomatoes, olive oil, and wines until as late a date as possible. Spain's fishing industry, the largest in Western Europe, received the right to fish in most European waters, but its catch was sharply restricted until 1995.

Spain's Costa del Sol

By 1989, when Spain's president served as president of the EU, it had truly proven its right to take its place within the European community. In 1995 and 2002, Spain's leaders again served as president. During this most recent presidency, Spain gave priority to the fight against terrorism, the enlargement of the EU, and economic and social reform.

Spain believes wholeheartedly in the power of the EU. In 2005, Spain was the first country to vote in support of a new EU charter that would streamline decision-making processes in the EU, allowing the EU to use its power more quickly and effectively.

Spanish businessman Jesús Banegas voted yes, because, he said, having Spain in the EU is good for business: "The obvious advantage of belonging to the EU is belonging to a bigger market where you can increase your business . . . and reduce costs." He added that belonging to the EU also forced Spaniards to grow after centuries of being on the fringe of Europe.

Before the vote, Prime Minister José Luis Rodríguez Zapatero told Spain: "We cannot miss the opportunity to be protagonists and set the course for all Europeans with a massive 'yes.'"

By saying yes to the EU, Spain is saying yes to the future.

A Calendar of Spanish Festivals

January: Reconquest Festival, when the people of Granada celebrate the Christian conquest of the Moors in 1492. On **Epiphany**, or **Three Kings Day**, children receive presents and candy in their shoes. In Spain, Santa Claus does not bring gifts, but the Three Wise Men do.

February: Madrid Carnival, a celebration that includes a masked ball, costumes, and the burial of a sardine, followed by a concert in the plaza mayor.

March: Valencia Fiesta, where people celebrate the coming of spring by burning effigies of winter demons. Bullfights and fireworks are also part of the fiesta.

April: Feria de Sevilla includes all-night flamenco dancing, bullfights, dancing in the streets, and horse riding. It may be the most celebrated event in Spain. **Moros y Christianos** is a battle reenactment with a circus-like atmosphere, while **Romeria** is the oldest festival in Spain. The **Pilgrimage of the Holy Visage** is a very important and popular event after Easter when 200,000 people holding pilgrimage canes walk to the Monastery of Santa Faz to worship at the shrine. They have picnic lunches, and a large arts and crafts market is held.

May: Festival de los Patios, when residents of Cordoba decorate their patios with cascades of flowers, and visitors wander from patio to patio. The **Fiesta de San Isidro** is a ten-day celebration of Madrid's patron saint; it includes parties, parades, bullfights, and dances.

June: Veranos de la Villa is celebrated in Madrid, with dancing, music, and concerts (often free of charge) that last all summer long. The **Feast of San Juan** is celebrated on the 23rd with bonfires on the beach, lasting all through the night. At midnight everyone rushes into the sea to symbolize the baptisms by John the Baptist. Some people also jump over bonfires to symbolically burn away their sins.

July: Running of the Bulls is one of the most famous events in Spain, where bulls are released into the streets.

August: La Tomatina (Battle of the Tomatoes), when tons of fruit are thrown between warring towns and villages in Valencia, followed by music and dancing.

November: All Saints Day, when relatives lay flowers on graves of the dead.

December: Christmas in Spain is celebrated with hogueras (bonfires), a pre-Christian tradition in observance of the winter solstice, the shortest day of the year. People jump over the fires as protection against illness in the coming year. Towns have Nacimientos, elaborate nativity scenes, and Christmas markets piled with fruit, marzipan, candles, decorations, and handmade gifts. Christmas dinner is eaten after midnight, and Christmas Day is spent at church, followed by more feasting. Swings are often set up in courtyards, and young people swing to the accompaniment of music. Christmas is followed by **Día de los Santos Inocentes (Day of the Holy Innocents)**, a "Fool's Day" when people do lots of silly things.

Spanish Omelet
(Tortilla Española)

Makes 3 servings

Ingredients
1 pound potatoes
1 cup plus 1 tablespoon olive oil
dash of salt
4 eggs

Directions
Wash and cut the potatoes into thin slices. Heat 1 cup of the oil in the pan on medium high, and add the potatoes and salt. Fry, stirring occasionally. When the potatoes look golden-brown, remove them from the pan and drain them on a paper towel. When well drained, place in a medium-sized bowl.

In a small bowl, beat the eggs well with a pinch of salt, and add to the potatoes. Mix well.

Reheat the oil, and once the oil is hot, add the potato and egg mixture. Shake the pan gently to move the mixture, so that none sticks to the bottom. Once the eggs seem solid, use the lid of the frying pan (or a large plate) to tip the omelet out of the pan, add a little more oil and slide the omelet in again, this time putting the less cooked side first into the pan. Cook until the omelet is golden on both sides.

Montecados
(Spanish cookies)

Makes 6 dozen

Ingredients
5 cups all-purpose flour
1 1/4 cups white sugar
1/4 teaspoon ground cinnamon
2 1/3 cups melted shortening
1/2 ounce anise extract
72 blanched almonds

Directions
Preheat the oven to 250°F (120°C).

Combine the flour, sugar, and cinnamon. Add the melted shortening and mix well. Stir in the anise and knead for 5 minutes. Roll into 1-inch balls and place 2 inches apart on an ungreased cookie sheet. Place a blanched almond on top of each cookie and push down slightly. Bake for 30 minutes. Cookies should remain pale. Let cookies cool on cookie sheet for 30 minutes.

Empanadas
(jam-filled cookies)

Makes 2 1/2 dozen

Ingredients
1/2 cup butter, softened
1 3-ounce package cream cheese
1 cup sifted all-purpose flour
1 cup fruit preserves
1/3 cup white sugar
1 teaspoon ground cinnamon

Directions
Day before: Cream butter and cream cheese together until smoothly blended. Beat in the flour. Shape dough into a smooth ball, wrap in foil or plastic wrap, and refrigerate overnight (or up to a week).

At Baking Time: Remove dough from refrigerator 30 minutes before using. Preheat the oven to to 375°F (190°C). Roll chilled dough thin. Cut with a round cookie cutter. Place small spoonful of jam in center of each circle and moisten edges with water. Fold circle in half and press edges together. Bake on ungreased cookie sheet 15 to 20 minutes. After you remove from the oven, immediately roll in sugar mixed with cinnamon.

Panellets
(Catalan potato cookies)

These cookies are traditionally served in Catalonia for All Saints Day on November 1.

Ingredients
1 pound small potatoes, scrubbed
1 cup almonds
1 cup white sugar
1 cup chopped almonds
1 egg white

Directions
Place potatoes in a saucepan with enough water to cover. Bring to a boil, and cook until tender, 20 to 30 minutes. When done, you can stab them with a fork, and they will fall off easily. Drain, cool slightly, and peel.

Preheat the oven to 350°F (175°C).

Place the almonds in a food processor, and grind to a fine powder. Add sugar to almonds, and process to mix. Transfer to a medium bowl. Add potatoes to the almond mixture, and mash together until it becomes a very thick paste. Roll into 1-inch balls, and roll the balls in chopped almonds. Place cookies on a baking sheet, and brush with egg white. Bake for 10 to 15 minutes in the preheated oven, until the tops are brown. Gently remove from the baking sheets, and cool on a plate in the refrigerator. Serve cold. They are supposed to be squishy when you eat them.

PROJECT AND REPORT IDEAS

Maps

- Draw a map of Spain showing its seventeen regional governments with their major cities. Don't forget to include the islands!
- Using papier-mâché, Play-Doh®, or flour and salt, make a map of Spain on a wooden board showing Spain's mountains, rivers, and three climate regions. Use food coloring or colored Play-Doh® to indicate the three regions.

Recipe for flour and salt dough:
4 cups flour
1 cup salt
1 1/2 cups hot water
2 teaspoons vegetable oil

Mix the salt and flour together, then gradually add the water until the dough becomes elastic. If your mixture turns out too sticky, simply add more flour. If it turns out too crumbly, simply add more water. Knead the dough until it's a good consistency. If you want colored dough, mix food coloring into the water before adding it to the dry ingredients. Or you can paint your creation after baking it at 200°F (93°C) for one hour.

Reports

- Write a well-researched paper on the history of Islam. Include in your report ways that Islam has influenced Spain's culture and nation.
- Write a cultural history of a Spanish city or town, including the people who founded the city, famous painters who have lived or worked there, important architecture such as churches or castles, and the city's modern festivals that celebrate its past.
- Write a report on the conflict between Muslims and Christians in the fifteenth century, and make comparisons with modern-day events around the world.

Group Activities

- Divide into two groups for a discussion of bullfighting. One group should present reasons why bullfighting might be considered cruel, while the other should offer reasons why this tradition could be seen as a cultural heritage.
- Role-play a scene between the Catholic monarchs Isabella and Ferdinand and the Muslim ruler, Emir Boabdil. Act out the perspectives and opinions of each individual.

CHRONOLOGY

8000–4000 BCE	Iberians move into Spain.
800 BCE	Celts arrive at the northern part of the Iberian Peninsula.
206 BCE	Roman Empire invades Spain.
4th century CE	Spain becomes Christian.
711–1248	Moors occupy the Iberian Peninsula.
854 CE	Madrid is established.
1085	Madrid's Muslim era ends.
1474	Marriage of Queen Isabella and King Ferdinand unite Castilian and Aragonese realms to create the original nation of Spain.
1492	Granada falls to Queen Isabella and King Ferdinand. Queen Isabella and King Ferdinand finance Christopher Columbus's trip to the New World.
1561	Madrid becomes permanent seat of the royal court.
1605	Part 1 of Miguel de Cervantes' novel *Don Quixote* is made available to the public. Part 2 was released in 1615.
1713	Spain cedes Gibralter to Great Britain.
1790s	The guitar is invented in Andalusia.
1888	World's Fair is held in Barcelona.
1929	Seville hosts the Latin American Exhibition.
1931	King Alfonso XIII abdicates the Spanish throne and Spain is declared a republic.
1942	Ferdinand Franco assumes complete control of Spain.
1958	Spain joins the Organisation for European Economic Co-operation.
1959	Basque Fatherland and Liberty (ETA) forms. Spain joins the World Bank.
1975	Ferdinand Franco dies and is succeeded by King Juan Carlos II.
1978	Spain's constitution creates the Cortes.
1986	Spain joins the European Community.
1995 and 2002	Spain's president serves as president of the European Union.
March 2004	Terrorist bomb on the Madrid train system kills two hundred.
2005	Spain is the first country to vote in favor of a new European charter.

FURTHER READING/INTERNET RESOURCES

Cervantes, Miguel de. *Don Quixote*. New York: Barnes and Noble Books, 2004.
Davis, Kevin A. *Look What Came from Spain*. New York: Watts Franklin, 2003.
Rogers, Lura. *Spain*. New York: Scholastic Library Publishing, 2001.
Williams, Mark R. *Story of Spain*. Chandler, Ariz.: Golden Era Books, 2004.

Travel Information

www.lonelyplanet.com/destinations/Europe/spain/
www.sispain.org/English/travelli

History and Geography

www.red2000.com/spain/primer/hist.html
www.countryreports.org/history/spaihist.htm
www.nationbynation.com/Spain/Geo.htm

Economic and Political Information

www.andalucia.com/spain/economy/home/.htm
countrystudies.us/spain/81.htm

Culture and Festivals

www.donquijote.org/culture/spain
www.spain-info.com/Culture

For More Information

Embassy of Spain in Canada
74 Stanley Avenue
Ottawa, ON K1M1P4 Canada

Embassy of Spain in the United States
2375 Pennsylvania Avenue NW
Washington, DC 10037
Tel.: 202-452-0100
spain@spainemb.org

Tourist Office of Spain
666 Fifth Avenue, No. 35
New York, NY 10103
Tel.: 212-265-8822
oetny@tourspain.es

U.S. Department of State
2201 C Street NW
Washington, DC 20520
Tel.: 202-647-4000

Glossary

abdicate: Resign a position.
abject: Allowing no hope of improvement or relief.
Allies: The group of countries who fought against the Axis powers in World War II.
apex: The narrowed or pointed end.
arcade: A covered passageway.
archipelago: A group or chain of islands.
arid: A region in which annual rainfall is less than 10 inches (25 cm.).

autonomous: Able to act independently.
Axis: The countries who were defeated in World War II, particularly Germany, Italy, and Japan.
barbarian: A member of a people whose culture and behavior were considered uncivilized.
blockade: An organized action to prevent people or goods from entering or leaving a place.

blocs: United groups of countries.

budget deficit: The amount by which projected spending exceeds projected income.

capital: Wealth in the form of money or property.

ceded: Gave up land rights or power to another country or group.

Cold War: The hostile, nonviolent relationship between the former Soviet Union and the United States, and their respective allies, between 1946 and 1989.

conquistadors: Spanish conquerors or adventurers.

conservatives: People who are reluctant to accept abrupt change, preferring instead to maintain things the way they are.

constitution: A country's written statement outlining the basic laws and principles by which it is governed.

customs duties: Taxes on goods entering the country.

discriminatory: Treating a person or group unfairly, especially because of prejudice about race, ethnicity, age, or gender.

excise: A tax on goods used domestically.

executive: The section of a country's government responsible for implementing decisions relating to laws.

galleys: Large ships used for war or trading in the Mediterranean Sea during the Middle Ages.

Gothic: Belonging to a style of architecture used in Western Europe from the twelfth to thefifteenth centuries, and characterized by pointed arches, flying buttresses, and high curved ceilings.

gross domestic product (GDP): The total value of all goods and services produced within a country in a year.

heavy industry: Manufacturing activities in which large amounts of raw materials and partially processed materials are made into products of higher value.

homogeneous: Having a uniform composition or structure.

inflation: An economic condition in which the supply of money or credit exceeds the amount of goods and services available for purchase.

infrastructure: A country's large-scale public systems, services, and facilities that are necessary for economic growth and development.

Inquisition: A thirteenth-century organization in the Roman Catholic Church formed to find, question, and sentence those who did not hold mainstream religious beliefs.

integration: Unity; the act of becoming one thing.

liberals: People who are tolerant of different views and standards, and who favor political reforms that extend democracy, distribute wealth more evenly, and protect personal freedoms.

mechanized: Equipped with machines.

Middle Ages: The period in European history between the end of the Roman Empire in the fifth century and the early fifteenth century.

mosque: A building in which Muslims worship.

nationalist: Extreme devotion to one nation and its interests above all others.

navigable: Deep and wide enough to allow safe passage of ships.

Neanderthal: A member of an extinct subspecies of humans that lived in Europe, northern Africa, and western Asia in the early Stone Age.

nomadic: Characteristic of a group of people who wander from place to place.

ostracized: Banished or excluded from society or from a particular group.

per capita: For each person.

plateau: A hill or mountain with a level top.

proportional representation: An electoral system in which each party's share of seats in government is the same as its share of all the votes cast.

quotas: Maximum numbers or quantities that are permitted or needed.

ratified: Officially approved.

referenda: Votes by the whole of an electorate on a specific question or questions put to it by a government.

republic: A form of government in which people elect representatives to exercise power for them.

secede: To formally withdraw from membership in an organization, state, or alliance.

separatist: In favor of breaking or staying away from a country or group.

service industries: Businesses that provide services for people (such as hospitals and restaurants).

solidarity: The act of standing together, presenting a united front.

sovereign: Self-governing and independent.

stagnancy: A state of inactivity in which no movement or development occurs.

stereotypes: Oversimplified, standardized images or ideas, often based on incorrect or incomplete information, held by a person or group about another person or group.

strategically: In a clever, useful way.

tariff: Tax levied by governments on goods, usually imports.

torrents: Swift-flowing, turbulent streams of water.

veto: The power of one branch of government to reject the legislation of another.

Western: Relating to countries, primarily in Europe and North and South America, whose culture and society are greatly influenced by traditions rooted in Greek and Roman culture and in Christianity.

World Bank: A specialized agency of the United Nations that guarantees loans to member nations for reconstruction and development purposes.

Index

PICTURE CREDITS

Corel: pp. 10–11, 13, 15, 16, 18, 20–21, 26, 30–31, 35, 36, 38–39, 40, 43, 46, 53, 54, 70–71, 73, 74

Used with permission of the European Communities: pp. 56–57, 59, 62, 65, 66

Photos.com: pp. 23, 24, 28, 32, 45, 50, 60, 68

Benjamin Stewart: pp. 48–49

BIOGRAPHIES

Rae Simons has written several nonfiction children's books, as well as children's and adult fiction. She speaks Spanish and enjoys learning about other countries and cultures.

SERIES CONSULTANT

Ambassador John Bruton served as Irish Prime Minister from 1994 until 1997. As prime minister, he helped turn Ireland's economy into one of the fastest-growing in the world. He was also involved in the Northern Ireland Peace Process, which led to the 1998 Good Friday Agreement. During his tenure as Ireland's prime minister, he also presided over the European Union presidency in 1996 and helped finalize the Stability and Growth Pact, which governs management of the euro. Before being named the European Commission Head of Delegation in the United States, he was a member of the convention that drafted the European Constitution, signed October 29, 2004.

The European Commission Delegation to the United States represents the interests of the European Union as a whole, much as ambassadors represent their countries' interests to the U.S. government. Matters coming under European Commission authority are negotiated between the commission and the U.S. administration.